Put Beginning Readers on the Right Track with
ALL ABOARD READING™

The All Aboard Reading series is especially designed for beginning readers. Written by noted authors and illustrated in full color, these are books that children really want to read—books to excite their imagination, expand their interests, make them laugh, and support their feelings. With fiction and nonfiction stories that are high interest and curriculum-related, All Aboard Reading books offer something for every young reader. And with four different reading levels, the All Aboard Reading series lets you choose which books are most appropriate for your children and their growing abilities.

Picture Readers
Picture Readers have super-simple texts, with many nouns appearing as rebus pictures. At the end of each book are 24 flash cards—on one side is a rebus picture; on the other side is the written-out word.

Station Stop 1
Station Stop 1 books are best for children who have just begun to read. Simple words and big type make these early reading experiences more comfortable. Picture clues help children to figure out the words on the page. Lots of repetition throughout the text helps children to predict the next word or phrase—an essential step in developing word recognition.

Station Stop 2
Station Stop 2 books are written specifically for children who are reading with help. Short sentences make it easier for early readers to understand what they are reading. Simple plots and simple dialogue help children with reading comprehension.

Station Stop 3
Station Stop 3 books are perfect for children who are reading alone. With longer text and harder words, these books appeal to children who have mastered basic reading skills. More complex stories captivate children who are ready for more challenging books.

In addition to All Aboard Reading books, look for All Aboard Math Readers™ (fiction stories that teach math concepts children are learning in school) and All Aboard Science Readers™ (nonfiction books that explore the most fascinating science topics in age-appropriate language).

All Aboard for happy reading!

For Maureen and Kathy—G.H.

To my sister Beverly—P.B.F.

Library of Congress Cataloging-in-Publication Data

Herman, Gail, 1959–
    Flower girl / by Gail Herman ; illustrated by Paige Billin-Frye.
      p.   cm. — (All aboard reading. Level 2)
    Summary: A young girl's lucky ring helps her be the perfect flower
girl in her sister's wedding.
    [1. Weddings—Fiction.   2. Sisters—Fiction.   3. Rings—Fiction.]
I. Billin-Frye, Paige, ill.   II. Title.   III. Series.
PZ7.H4315F1   1996
[E]—dc20   95-43011
                                             CIP
                                             AC

ISBN 0-448-41108-3   2008 Printing

Flower Girl

By **Gail Herman**
Illustrated by **Paige Billin-Frye**

Grosset & Dunlap • New York

Chapter 1

We are at a fancy place for dinner—

my mom and dad,

my sister, Donna,

her boyfriend, Bill,

and me.

Yours truly.

I do not like this place.

It is way too dark.

The food is yucky.

And if we don't leave soon,

I will miss my favorite TV show.

I rub my lucky ring.

"Please let the check come,"

I say over and over.

"What are you saying?"

Donna asks me.

"Um…nothing!"

I say quickly.

Donna turns to Mom and Dad.

"We have something to say."

She takes Bill's hand.

<u>Boring</u>, I think.

I go back to rubbing my lucky ring.

All at once,

I hear a clank.

Mom has dropped her fork.

Dad is crying.

I missed something.

Something big!

"What, what, what!"

I shout.

"What did you say?"

Donna smiles.

"Bill and I are getting married.

And we want you

to be our flower girl."

Donna! Married!

Me a flower girl!

Donna is my favorite person

in the whole world.

I am so happy.

I look at my ring.

This really is a lucky day.

Chapter 2

Today Donna takes me to the mall

on flower-girl business.

We are looking for a dress.

We go into a store.

There are so many dresses!

Dresses with bows.

Dresses with ruffles.

Dresses that go all the way

down to the floor.

I like them all!

Then I see it.

The best dress of all.

It's pink and shimmery.

Just like my lucky ring!

But another girl tries it on.

Oh, no!

I rub my lucky ring.

"Don't let her buy it,"

I say.

The dress is too big for her.

My lucky ring has done it again!

Then I try on the dress.

It is the dress of my dreams.

I am going to be

the best flower girl ever!

Chapter 3

It seems like forever,

but at last it is the day of the wedding.

All the people are in the church.

I squeeze Donna's hand.

She looks so pretty.

Just like a fairy princess.

Mom kisses her.

I peek inside.

There are aunts, uncles,

cousins, friends—

so many people.

They all will be looking at me!

"Good luck," says Donna

because I go first.

I gulp.

My dress is perfect.

But what if I'm not?

What if I trip?

What if I sneeze?

What if I am not

the best flower girl ever?

My tummy drops.

Just like it does

when I go high in a swing

I start to rub my lucky ring.

Donna has a funny look on her face.

She must be scared too.

I hold out my ring.

Maybe she would like to rub it.

"Get that thing off!"

she says.

"What? What?" I say.

"That ring!

You can't wear that ring,

Donna says.

"But I have to,"

I tell her.

"I never take off my lucky ring."

"Mom!"

Donna shouts.

Mom comes over.

"Please," she says to me.

"That ring does not go

with your fancy dress.

Please take it off."

I start to say it is my lucky ring.

But Mom crosses her arms.

It is no use.

She means business.

And I do not want

to make Donna unhappy.

I take off my ring.

The music starts.

I gulp again.

Now I am <u>really</u> scared.

But I have an idea.

Chapter 4

I hold my basket of flowers tight.

And here I go—

past uncles, aunts,

cousins, and friends.

I hear lots of oohs and aahs.

I walk to my spot.

There!

I did it—

and just right too!

Bill is already there.

So is his brother, Mike,

the best man.

Then Donna steps up.

The wedding starts.

There is lots of stuff about love.

Blah, blah, blah.

Boring.

Then I hear a gasp.

It is Bill.

"Where is the ring?"

he hisses.

His brother turns red.

"I left it home,"

he says in a whisper.

No ring for Donna?

This is bad!

But wait—I can help.

I take my lucky ring out of the basket.

It helped me.

And now it can help Donna too.

"Here is a ring," I say.

I smile at Donna.

Uh-oh.

She doesn't smile back.

She is too surprised.

But then she grins.

She is glad I have the ring!

I give the ring to Mike.

Mike gives it to Bill.

Bill puts it on Donna's finger.

Donna and Bill are married!

Donna wears the ring
when she dances,

and cuts the cake,

and says good-bye
to all the uncles, aunts,
cousins, and friends.

Last of all she

says good-bye to me.

"Thank you for saving the day,"

she says....

"You really are

the perfect flower girl."